For my family of relatives (Jonah, Liam, McKenna, Mom & Brian) for
all of our Vancouver walks. And for my family of friends (Christina,
Tiffany, Lori, Sheena & Jill) for all of our writing talks — KLW

To Christianne Hayward, for pointing me in the right direction — CL

Text copyright © 2009 by Kari-Lynn Winters
Illustrations copyright © 2009 by Christina Leist

Released in the US in 2010.

Cataloguing and publication data available from the British Library.

Book design by Elisa Gutiérrez • The text of this book is set in Leticia Bumstead.

10 9 8 7 6 5 4 3 2 1 • Printed and bound in China on ancient-forest-friendly paper.

The publisher wishes to thank the Government of Canada and Canadian
Heritage for their financial support through the Canada Council for the
Arts, the Book Publishing Industry Development Program (BPIDP) and the
Association for the Export of Canadian Books (AECB). The publisher also
wishes to thank the Government of the Province of British Columbia for
the financial support it has extended through the Book Publishing Tax
Credit program and the British Columbia Arts Council.

Manufactured by Meiya-Yanzhong Printing   Manufactured in Shanghai, P.R., China in September 2009   Job number: scc-116

LIBRARY AND ARCHIVES CANADA
CATALOGUING IN PUBLICATION

Winters, Kari-Lynn, 1969-
   On my walk / Kari-Lynn
Winters ; illustrated by Christina
Leist.
Poems.
ISBN 978-1-896580-61-6
   I. Leist, Christina II. Title.
PS8645.I58O5 2009 jC811'.6 C2009-904158-8

Canada Council   Conseil des Arts
for the Arts   du Canada

BRITISH
COLUMBIA
ARTS COUNCIL

Kari-Lynn Winters

On My Walk

· TRADEWIND · BOOKS ·

VANCOUVER · LONDON

illustrated by **Christina Leist**

my Summer walk,

I hear a horse,

clippity-clop,
clippity-clop,

and catch some rain,

And some rain?

On my run, my summer run,

frop, frop,

clippity-clop, clippity-clop,

all the way home.